PUFFIN BOOKS

MOULDY'S ORPHAN

It was bitter cold, walking home from school along the towpath, but then how good it was when they all crowded into their cottage and warmed themselves by the fire or rocked the baby's cradle until Dad came in and Mum gave them all their tea.

So Mouldy dreamed about how a poor orphan from the London streets would enjoy it too. Mouldy knew all about orphans because of a terribly sad book she had been reading called *Froggy's Little Brother*. If she found one, she knew just what she would do. She would bring him home and sit him on the rag rug, and then she'd rub and warm his poor bare feet, and give him a mug of hot tea and a slice of toast and dripping. Then she would promise him, 'you can stay here for ever and ever!' and how *happy* he would be!

The only snag was, there weren't any orphans where Mouldy lived, and she didn't know where to get one. But the golden opportunity came when kind Mr Gerald took the schoolchildren for the best treat of their lives – a trip to Oxford on a train to see a pantomime – and to crown it all, Mouldy found a real orphan of her own.

Triumphantly, delightedly, Mouldy took him home, but Mum and Dad didn't play their parts right at all. They said they had too many mouths to feed, and the orphan boy couldn't stay, but even that didn't mean Mouldy was defeated.

Gillian Avery was born in Reigate, Surrey. At seventeen she became the first woman reporter on the *Surrey Mirror*, but decided against a journalistic career and went into publishing, where she met her husband, an authority on Victorian literature.

Mouldy's Orphan

Gillian Avery

Illustrated by Faith Jaques

PUFFIN BOOKS

PUFFIN BOOKS

Published by the Penguin Group
Penguin Books Ltd, 27 Wrights Lane, London W8 5TZ, England
Penguin Books USA Inc., 375 Hudson Street, New York, New York 10014, USA
Penguin Books Australia Ltd, Ringwood, Victoria, Australia
Penguin Books Canada Ltd, 10 Alcorn Avenue, Toronto, Ontario, Canada M4V 3B2
Penguin Books (NZ) Ltd, 182–190 Wairau Road, Auckland 10, New Zealand

Penguin Books Ltd, Registered Offices: Harmondsworth, Middlesex, England

First published by William Collins Sons & Co. Ltd 1978
Published in Puffin Books 1981
9 10 8

Printed in England by Clays Ltd, St Ives plc
Set in Monotype Baskerville

Contents

NOTE

You must imagine yourself in the Oxfordshire countryside of ninety years ago, when the cottage people very often did not move more than a few miles from their home in the whole of their lives; when there were trains, but otherwise only feet or horses to carry them over the country lanes between the village and the market town.

Working hours were long and money was short, especially for the farm-workers like Mouldy's father, but they did not think of themselves as really poor. The really poor were the ragged and destitute, and the children without parents and without homes, who were still to be found roaming the city streets.

But for all of these, anything was better than the workhouse, which was all the State then offered to people who could not earn a living.

Froggy's Little Brother is a real book, written in 1875 by an author who called herself 'Brenda'.

G.A.

I

Canal Row

"Our Billy" led the way home, stopping now and then to yell at his sisters to get a move on. Mouldy and May and little Flo, stumbling along the canal towpath behind him, could see his breath smoking in the cold air. Then he would turn and push on. The path was greased with mud. It was like the fat in Mum's frying pan when it was going cold, Mouldy thought dreamily, as she slithered and tried to keep Flo alongside her. It was difficult. There was hardly room on the path for three side by side, but it was one of the rules. They must all come home from school together, all four of them, and Mouldy must never let go of Flo's and May's hands while they walked by the canal.

Flo grizzled. She wanted to be home, but she didn't want to hurry. The scarf that her mother criss-crossed over her and round her when she sent her off to school was trailing in the mud, because Mouldy didn't understand how to roll her up in it. Her nose was running and she tried to lick it away but her tongue wasn't long enough, so she just wailed and dragged behind. May, older than Flo by two years, pulled forward, dodging the dried stalks by the water's edge. You might say that she was the one who was taking them all along. Mouldy was the oldest, but Mouldy was a dreamer.

They had reached the bridge now, the one that took them over the canal to the proper road on the other side. There was no sign of Billy though they could hear his boots in the distance.

"He'll go telling Mum about it the first," complained May. "All because you won't hurry, Mouldy. It isn't fair." Then she shouted after Billy, "You'll get a tanning for going on like that." It was the only satisfaction in it.

"I want my tea," snivelled Flo. She was falling over her scarf-end now; it was drabbled and muddy where she had trodden on it. She rubbed her nose along her coat sleeve and then tried to pick up the scarf. She had started school only that autumn and she wasn't yet used to the long walk home.

The dark was coming down quickly now. The wintry sun had long ago disappeared leaving just pink sky behind the bare elms ahead. The hedges pressed in on both sides. You could easily make yourself frightened thinking of what was behind them.

"Shall I tell you a story?" said Mouldy. Flo gave a howl and pulled forward.

"It wasn't going to be one of *those*," said Mouldy, offended. "It was one about an orphan."

Flo gave another howl. "Don't let her, May. Make her stop it."

"Mum'll tan you too," said May. "I'll tell on you, Mouldy! She said you wasn't never to go telling her about ghosts and goblins and bogies."

"Orphans isn't them," Mouldy tried to explain. "Orphans is children. Ones that hasn't got fathers and mothers because they're dead."

Flo began to shriek. "I don't want to hear about dead 'uns. I want Mum." She broke into a run now, stumbling in the ruts, trying to pull Mouldy on. But running along cart-tracks in the dusk is difficult when you are holding hands. She tripped and fell flat. There was a second's hush while she drew in her breath to yell.

And yell she did all the way home. Even when at last they saw the lights of Canal Row twinkling ahead of them, reflected back from the dark waters of the canal – that cheerful sight which usually made them all break into a happy trot at the thought of tea and fire – Flo kept it up, if anything rather louder. Faces came to the windows, curtains were pulled aside.

"You'll catch it, Mouldy," said May with relish. She wrenched herself out of Mouldy's grip (it was all right now that home was in sight) and trotted on towards the last house in the row of cottages that stood there by the canal.

Mum was at the door and pounced. "I heard her. All the way down the lane. Fit to scare the crows. And just look at her."

Flo hurled herself at her mother. "I fell down. I don't want to hear about dead 'uns. Make Mouldy stop, Mum." She might as well make the most of her crying now that Mum's mind was on her.

"Did our Billy tell you, Mum?" May clamoured. "Did he? Well, then, can we go?"

Her mother brushed her aside. "It'll have to wait till Daddy comes home, you know that as well as I do. Nobody's going to talk about dead 'uns," she told Flo, pulling the scarf off her. Then she drew in her breath with exasperation, as she looked at the bedraggled, sodden end. "You haven't been and gone and lost that child's safety-pin again, Moll! I told you it was the last one in the house and to take care when you put it in. You haven't got the sense of a rabbit, that you haven't."

"My hands are cold, I'm cold all over," hiccuped Flo. "And I don't like it being dark and I don't like Mouldy's stories."

"She isn't going to tell stories. As for the dark, it's here till tomorrow morning. Now stop that noise or you'll wake the baby. There, now you have. For pity's sake, Moll, give the cradle a rock, and keep young Georgie from falling into the fire. And May, you come over and help Billy make the toast. Otherwise we'll have Daddy in and tea not ready."

The wet clothes were stripped off Flo and she sat on her stool by the fire while her mother rubbed at her hands, red and purple and swollen with cold. At first she cried louder, because it hurt so when her cold hands started to get warm. But her noise turned to sniffs, and then to a catch in her breathing. She was home, where she wanted to be. There was toast and dripping for tea and Mum was loving her.

Mouldy (the children called her that, because they said her hair was like mouldy hay; really she was Moll or Mollie) pushed at the wooden cradle with her foot and held Georgie by the tail of his skirts with a limp hand. Her mind wasn't on them. Her mind never was where it should be. She was thinking how comfortable it was to be here. If she brought an orphan off the London streets, just wouldn't he love it.

The fire was good and red; there was a savoury smell from the pot that hung over it;

the brass candlesticks shone (the Kippinses were the only family in the Row to have brass ones); the table was spread for tea. She would bring her orphan in, she would sit him on the rag rug and rub his poor bare feet warm, and put a mug of tea in one of his hands and a slice of toast and dripping in the other.

"There," she would say, "you get warm and then you can go upstairs and our Billy and Georgie'll make room for you in their bed, and Mum'll give you a hot brick wrapped in flannel like she does when we're ill, and you can stay here for ever and ever." Tears rose in her eyes as she thought about it, and her grip slackened on Georgie's skirts. With a twist he wriggled away and hurled himself at Billy.

"Gimme," he shouted, and clutched at the toasting-fork. The bread fell into the fire. Billy gave a shout and banged at Georgie who howled, and the baby woke with an angry wail as Mouldy's foot stopped rocking him. There was the sound of heavy boots outside and somebody scraping the mud off. Then the latch was raised.

2

"Can we go?"

There was a hush, only the baby wailed now.
Three pairs of eyes — Mouldy's and Billy's and
May's — shot anxious looks at him; was he in
the mood to be asked for favours? He nodded
at their mother; then, standing on the old sack
just inside the door, stooped to unlace his
muddy boots. In stockinged feet he padded
across the floor to the door at the other side.

"Will *you* ask him, Mum?" said Billy in a
whisper, under cover of the splashing noises
from the back scullery.

"You'll have to do it yourself. Wait till he's
had his tea, though."

They could smell the soap when their father
came back, his hair sticking in spikes where it
had got wet. He shuffled his feet into the slippers

that had been warming by the fire and then lowered himself into the chair by the table. The children scraped up their stools over the floor. Billy put the mound of toast on the table and Mum ladled out the vegetables into seven bowls, each with a bit of pink bacon on top, and poured out the tea.

"Fetch my pipe, Mollie my girl," said their father at last, clattering down the huge tea-cup (it had a bar across it, to stop his moustaches getting wet).

Billy tweaked at her as she passed. "You ask, you're the eldest."

Mouldy reached up to the mantelpiece for one of the clay pipes. Breathing hard with the effort not to break it this time, she put it on the cloth by her father, and then fetched the tobacco jar. Billy gave her another nudge. "Go on," he said hoarsely.

"Billy and May and me," said Mouldy with a rush. "We was wondering . . . well, you know Mr Gerald up at the Vicarage? The one that's the brother of Mrs Donaldson? Well, he's at college in Oxford and he's been staying at the Vicarage with the Vicar and Mrs Donaldson and sometimes he comes into school and teaches us songs (at least, he has twice) and he says (well, he did today) . . ."

May could bear it no longer and cut in. "Mr Gerald's going to take the school to Oxford for a treat to see the pantomime and can we go?"

Nothing was said. Their father's fingers stuffed tobacco into the pipe. "Fetch me a light," he told Mouldy. She lit a taper at the fire. Sometimes she managed, sometimes the draught blew it out before she ever got it to him. This time it worked. There were puffing noises, then he blew it out.

"Who's going?" he asked.

"Everybody except the babies." May nodded at Flo. "And it'll be free, and Teacher's going, and Mr Gerald and one of Mr Gerald's friends and Kitty Drew (that's the pupil teacher). And we're to go by train from the junction — that's why the little ones can't go, because it's too far for them to walk."

"Go by *train*!" Billy repeated ecstatically.

"And then march to the theatre. And it's a huge place, hundred times bigger than the schoolroom, and so bright. And there'll be fancy costumes and people singing and people being funny. And Mr Gerald says we might have *oranges* too."

"I want an orange," wailed Flo.

"*You're* not going," said May quenchingly.

George joined in. "Want an orange, I do."

"Nobody's going," said their mother sharply. "Not unless there's hush. I told them, Jim," she said to her husband, "that you must say. I don't know, I'm sure. It's a long way, it sounds fair mad to me. All that walk on a winter's night and a train, and then back late in the dark."

"He's chosen a night when there's a moon," said May. "He told us so."

Clouds of smoke were now filling the room. "Do *you* want to go?" their father asked Mouldy.

"Want to go?" Mouldy gaped at him.

"You don't usually want to do like the rest. Mope round by yourself, that's what it seems."

Mouldy groped for the words that would say what she felt. "It's a *story* – acted on the stage. There's something called a transformation scene." (She said it very slowly and carefully.) "Where everything changes into something different. Like magic."

"Like magic!" said Billy scornfully. "You and your stories! She's brought her *book* home from school again. Her *book*!" He repeated it with disgust.

His father pushed down at the pipe with his thumb. "You lay off Mollie. She's a bit of a dreamer, but she's all right. Come here, our Moll. Come over, bring your stool."

With a heavy hand he rumpled her hair, the wiry strands that never looked tidy, that stuck out in wisps like a haystack that the cows had got at – as the children at school were always telling her. "Is it your orphan book again? That poor boy in London town? We could do a sight better for him here in Canal Row. You bring it over and read us a bit."

"Now then, Mollie," said her mother. "Don't get that excited that you go knocking things over."

"Can we *go* then?" demanded Billy.

"You can go," said their father. "There doesn't seem harm in it."

There was a trembling sigh from all of them. Daddy was in one of his best moods. The fire was warm, the dark was outside, they were full of toast and dripping. They sat hunched on their stools while Mouldy's voice droned on. *Froggy's Little Brother* the story was called. It was in the Sunday School library. People could sometimes take books home, though mostly they were used when Teacher read aloud. *Froggy* was all about boys who hadn't got any mother or father and were hungry and cold in London. So hungry and cold that one of them died. It wasn't like that in Canal Row. Everybody had enough to eat there. And if the book got too sad you could always think about that Christmas treat: a train (two trains, if you counted the coming back), Oxford (none of them had ever been there), a theatre, and oranges.

In bed, Mouldy couldn't make up her mind. She always told herself stories before she went to sleep. Should it be a story about going to the theatre in Oxford? Or her usual one of bringing an orphan home, a little, thin, starved, cold one in rags like Froggy or his brother Ben, and feeding him and warming him and comforting him? She still hadn't decided when she fell asleep.

3

On the train!

Three weeks later, even the march to the junction was exciting. It had been damp and rainy all December, but now, in January, there had been days of frost; the ground was iron-hard and the puddles crackled as the children stepped on them.

The Canal Row children were to walk together to the high road and there wait for the party that was coming from Stradling, the mother-village where the church and the school were. Stradling was a large village and there would be nearly fifty children besides the fourteen from Canal Row. Then there were three miles to tramp to the station where they were to catch the late afternoon train. But who minded that with all that lay ahead?

Mr Gerald made them all sing. He had been teaching them marching songs. *John Brown's Body*, they all shouted, and *Men of Harlech* and *The Lincolnshire Poacher*. Their boots clattered on the frosty road and they tried to shout louder and louder to startle the rooks that flapped up and down the furrows, and to carry their voices across the bare fields to the farms that lay behind the trees.

At the junction the oil lamps had just been lit. The children had often been to the railway line to watch for trains, but few of them had ever been on one, and certainly none of the Canal Row lot. If you wanted to go to a town you walked along the field paths to Brackley. Sometimes you went on the carrier's van to Banbury. But mostly you stayed at home, just trudging along the canal between the Row and Stradling for school and church.

So when the train came thundering in, within inches of where they stood, hissing and puffing, even the boys drew back, and the girls had their hands over their ears. They huddled together like a flock of sheep, and the teachers and Mr Gerald had hard work to sort them out and push them into the different carriages.

Mouldy couldn't get over the speed, the way the darkening fields went flashing by. She wished they could go on rushing through the evening for ever. Did birds feel like this – flying on and on and on so easily? She was roused by a hefty pinch from May.

"You're being talked to."

Dazed, Mouldy looked around her. Opposite, in the crowded carriage where the children sat squeezed up together, legs dangling, was Mr Gerald's friend, the young man who was helping take them on the treat. She gaped at him, her mouth hanging open in the way Mum was always telling her not to.

"I was just saying, is this your first visit to Oxford?"

As usual, May managed to chip in first. "None of us has ever been. Mouldy and our Billy's been to Brackley, though."

"Is Oxford bigger than Brackley?" Mouldy could find words now that she had been given a lead.

"A lot bigger. Full of really big buildings – colleges and libraries and churches."

"Big as London?"

"Oh, steady on!" said Mr Gerald's friend. "London's the biggest city in the world. Oxford's just . . ."

While he groped to explain Mouldy interrupted. "Has Oxford got *slums* then?"

Mr Gerald's friend was startled. "I daresay. Yes, of course it has. Every city has slums."

"And *orphans*? Poor children that haven't got homes?"

"It's *Froggy's Little Brother*!" said May with disgust. "That's what she's on about. Ol' Mouldy reads *books*. Even if you take them away from her she won't stop thinking about them."

Mouldy took no notice. "Will we see slums then? Is it like what they say? Cursing and swearing and drinking, and children with no one to belong to?"

"Oh give over, Mouldy, do," May complained. "As if we hadn't heard enough about Froggy."

Mouldy would have had to stop in any case, for the train was at a station picking up more passengers. It hardly looked like a station,

more like a cattle shelter, but there were enough people getting in. Children pushed into the carriage, chattering, jostling, so that you could no longer talk to the people on the other side. The Canal Row lot were kicking furtively at the newcomers and then looking the other way.

"Call that a station! Bit of old iron more like."

"Reckon they're going the same place as us," said somebody.

"*We're* going to Oxford."

"So are we, then."

"*We're* going to the pantomime."

"So are we, so there."

"There's eighty-nine of us," said one of the new crowd. "And that's not counting teachers."

The Canal Row lot kept quiet. They couldn't beat that. "Where did you come from, then? Fields?" said someone at last. "Didn't seem anything else."

"We walked all the way from Woodstock. It's a *town*. It hasn't got a station – it's going to have, though. A good big one, better'n yours, I daresay."

"It's going to take some sorting out," Mouldy heard Mr Gerald's friend say from the other side of the mob of standing children who lurched this way and that as the train swung on. "I hope you know all their faces."

It did take a lot of sorting out. There seemed to be no end to the counting and arranging of them in twos as they stood under the lamps at Oxford station, with the teachers and Mr Gerald and his friend running up and down the lines, while the porters tried to get past with their trucks, and the boys in front kept starting to lead the procession off, and the Other Lot (as they all now called the Woodstock children) shouting at them rudely from a few yards away, and the Stradling lot trying to shout back without the teachers noticing.

After that, the march to the theatre and the finding of their seats was easy, because everybody was daunted by the size and the noisiness of Oxford, the lights and the jostling crowds in the theatre, and tried to keep together.

They all remembered different things about the pantomime. Mouldy didn't laugh at the funny bits like some of them. She just held hard to the bench and marvelled – at the way the people down on the stage far below spoke in rhyme, at the way the dancers went on the tips of their toes, at the clothes that glittered and gleamed, at the magic way things changed so one minute there was snow falling, and then it all changed into bright summer and leaves came on the trees as you looked, and flowers grew on the stage.

Nor was that the end of it. There was more snow because of some wicked ugly little dwarf who stood waving his stick and frightening everybody and it all seemed to be ending badly. Then, just as you were giving up hope, it changed again. There was a dazzle of lights of every colour, and a little girl dressed in shining silver came floating down from the sky in a bubble and waved her wand, and the people around changed in front of your eyes. Their clothes fell to the ground and there they were, quite different – clowns, dancers, men in masks, more and more of them crowding on to the stage . . .

4

Benjy

"Come along, Mouldy, do." Someone was shaking her shoulder. "Teacher's waiting and she's getting that cross."

Dazed, Mouldy clattered down the steps with the others. There were torrents of people pouring out of the theatre and it was hard to see which party you belonged to. Outside, the teachers and Mr Gerald tried to gather the flock together. It was not easy; they kept on getting mixed up with other children and pushed out of place by the crowds. Vaguely, Mouldy noticed him, a little boy in the shadow of a nearby wall standing and watching. He edged nearer to her.

"Been to the panto?"

She nodded; blurred memories of all the

lights and the costumes seemed to be whirling past her; she could still hardly see straight. "Are you the Other Lot?" she said, remembering the insults and kicks and tweaks that had been exchanged. "The ones on the train with us?"

"On the train?" The boy gave a whistle. "I'se *seen* trains. But where'd I have money to go on 'em?"

"It was a school treat. They took us. We didn't pay."

"Don't go to school," he said triumphantly.

Mouldy marvelled. "We wouldn't be allowed not. Somebody'd come round and tell Mum."

The boy shrugged. "There isn't nobody to tell. I keeps out of all their way. Nobody knows about me."

Mouldy was coming out of her fog. Now she noticed his matted hair, his raggy clothes (she could see his knees through his trousers), the boots that were far too big for him and the soles coming away from the uppers. "Are you an *orphan*?" she said in a quavering voice. "Someone with no mother and father? Nowhere to live?" She was fumbling in the paper bag

NEW THEATRE

GRACE JEWELL

PERFORMING IN

GRAND

PANTOM

they had given her in the theatre, for the orange and the bun she had saved to take back to Flo and Georgie. "Would you like these?"

"Would I like them? Cor!"

"Your name isn't Froggy is it?" said Mouldy, watching him take huge bites at the bun. Of course she really knew it couldn't be, the question just slipped out.

"Froggy? That's not a *name*. Benjy's my name."

Mouldy nearly sobbed with excitement. "Benjy? But that was what *his* brother was called. Froggy's Little Brother Ben!"

Somebody gave her a dig from behind. "Come *on*, we're going now and we've to hurry because of the train. And keep together and don't straggle, Teacher says; they don't want us mixed up with the Other Lot."

But at Oxford station there was such a press of children that it would have been impossible not to get mixed up with the Other Lot. Luckily everybody was so tired that they didn't want to fight any more. They stood limply waiting, longing to be sitting down and wishing that there wasn't that long walk back from the junction. Then, when the train came, they couldn't even sit down, not in their carriage, because some of the Other Lot had pushed on ahead and grabbed the seats.

Wearily they stood between the knees on either side, swaying to and fro, sometimes thrown into people's laps; not excited any more, not talking even. Besides, in the scramble they'd got separated; the Canal Row set weren't all together, they were mixed up with Stradlings, many of whom were almost strangers.

At last the junction came and they tumbled on to the platform and drooped in a shivering huddle, while they were counted for the last time. There seemed to be difficulty getting the numbers right.

"There's nobody *missing*, at any rate," said Mr Gerald's friend. "You must have forgotten to count one of us grown-ups before, me, probably. I'm the odd one out. We'd better hurry them back before they drop in their tracks with tiredness."

They didn't sing now. They just trotted along the road as fast as they could, lurching and skidding on the frozen puddles, Mr Gerald at the back urging on the laggards. Everything seemed to be crackling with frost, and overhead a huge white moon hung in the bright, cold sky.

The Canal turn came at last. The Stradling children had a mile more to march along the main turnpike road. Canal Row was a mile, but down the side road.

"Off you go, you Canals," shouted Mr Gerald. "No dilly-dallying, mind. And keep together. Are they all there, Miss Dickson?"

Teacher, in front, halted the procession and looked back into the shadows. "What did I tell you to say at the end of your treat?"

"Thank you very much, Mr Gerald," they called back over their shoulders, those of them that hadn't run on already. And then they all disappeared up the lane. But they didn't keep together. Everybody forgot the rules; they just wanted to get home as fast as they could, out of the cold, out of the dark. Of course Mouldy was last. She always was. Billy and May had got there before her and were crouching in front of the fire which their mother was banking up with ash ready for the morning. But it wasn't just Mouldy who pushed into the cottage. There was someone behind her.

"Come on," she said to him. "Mum'll make you warm and we'll all look after you. It's Froggy's little brother," she announced triumphantly. "He's called Benjy and he's an orphan."

5

The trouble that Mouldy brought

"She brought him home last night?" said the other children, incredulous. "Ol' Mouldy did?" They turned to stare at Mouldy who was skulking behind May in the frosty churchyard, pale-faced and red-eyed. "What did your Mum say then? What about your Dad?"

"Mum said she sometimes thought Mouldy was weak in the head, but she didn't know she was that bad," said May importantly.

"And how about your Dad?"

"Dad was in the Noah's Ark, like he always is Saturday nights."

"When he got home then?"

"He said we was to keep him for the night and then we'd have to see the Vicar and Mr Gerald and have him took away."

"But how did she get him here?"

"I don't know. How did you, Mouldy?"

Mouldy just shook her head. "I brought him on the train. Nobody noticed. It was dark and there was lots of people." She gave a hiccup. She had been crying most of the night and most of the morning too, and she still couldn't get back her breath.

"Where's he now, then?"

"Back home, nursing the baby. He loves babies, he said so. He said he had a baby sister once before his Mum died." At the thought of it, tears started streaming down Mouldy's face again.

"Who does he belong to?"

"He doesn't belong nowhere," said Mouldy passionately. "He lived on a canal boat once but he can't hardly remember. Then his Mum died, and the baby died, and the boat went away up the canal and he was left behind in Oxford, so he just sleeps rough in the town or in the fields by the canal down there. And if anybody tries to make him go to school or anything he runs away. But mostly they leave him alone, he says. He says he doesn't mind much, but it's cold in the winter. And he loves our baby, already he does, and he'd like to stay." Her shoulders started heaving as she thought about it.

The church bell, which had been tolling for the latecomers, stopped. The children, huddled behind the huge old yew tree on the far side of the church, out of the way of interfering grown-ups, looked at each other uneasily in the sudden silence.

"Best go," said one. "Everybody'll be in their places now and Teacher'll be on the look-out. You'd better stop making that noise, Mouldy, she won't half have it in for you if you don't."

But sitting in the front pews with the other school children, Mouldy couldn't stop crying. Her lips moved, but it wasn't with the words of the psalm, which she couldn't see, anyway, because her eyes were swimming. She just had to move them so that Teacher and Kitty Drew – who saw everything – couldn't say she wasn't attending.

She cried because she had thought she was

bringing Benjy to a house where everybody would welcome him and love him. And now he couldn't stay, and he would have to go back to his cold fields, and scrounge for food, and there wouldn't be a baby for him to nurse – nobody to take any notice of him at all.

Sunday dinner in Canal Row usually was a comfortable meal. The cottage had always been swept and polished the day before so there wasn't any cleaning, and even Mum took things more easily. Everybody felt peaceful. There was roast meat and gravy, and a pudding with currants in it, and with the children's father around they all held their hush; Billy didn't tease, nor May boss them all.

But today it was different. They were all quiet, certainly, but they were uneasy, looking at this stranger among them. There had hardly been time to speak to Benjy, even if anybody knew what to say to him. They had squashed up to make room for him at the table, and Mouldy had Flo in her lap so that he could have her stool.

He looked so different from the others with

their mouse-coloured hair and their rosy cheeks. Benjy had black hair and brown eyes and brown skin. He didn't seem to know how to use a knife and fork, but with furtive looks round the table, popped things into his mouth with his fingers. And Mum, who would never have allowed it in the other children, let him be. They stared at him, all except Mouldy, who drooped over her plate. She didn't even want any pudding.

"That's our Billy's trousers he's wearing," said Flo at last. "Mum, our Mouldy's holding me that tight I can't breathe. Can't I get down? Is he going to stay here for ever and ever? Won't I *never* have my stool back?"

"I'm going along to see the Vicar this afternoon. While you're all at Sunday school. And you'd better run along now, quick sharp, or you'll be late."

"Is *he* coming with us?" said Flo.

"He's going to come to the Vicarage with me."

"Will he be there when we come back then?"

"I don't know, and that's the end of it. So get your coats on, and Flo, you come here while I pin your scarf round you."

"Perhaps they'll take him off to the work-house," suggested May brightly. "That's where people get took as hasn't any homes."

Up till then Benjy had been quite quiet, accepting the clothes they had put on him and the food that had been set before him. But now he gave a shriek and pushed his way towards the door. He couldn't get out. Billy was leaning his back against it as he struggled to lace up his boots, but Benjy hammered his fists on it.

"I'm not going to no work'us. I've run away all the time from those as wanted to take me there. What did you go bringing me here for?" he shouted savagely at Mouldy. "You said you was taking me to a proper home where there was a baby. I didn't ask to come. You said come."

Mouldy flung herself hysterically at her mother. "You can't let him go to the work-house." She butted Mum's apron front. "You can't, you can't. It's prison, that's what it is. I've seen the one in Brackley. He'll die if he goes there."

Her mother seized her shoulder. "Mollie Kippins, that's no way to be carrying on. All this trouble you've brought on us and him too, and now us trying to get it all straight, and you bellowing and roaring like nobody's business! What an example to the little ones! You should have thought of all this before you did such a stupid silly thing."

Mr Kippins spoke. "He won't go to Brackley House, you can set your mind easy on that. They wouldn't have him, him not being from these parts."

"But where then?" said Mouldy frantically. "Look, he's trying to run off now." (Benjy was indeed rattling and tugging at the latch, though he couldn't get out as the solid mass of Billy was heavily against the door.)

Mr Kippins came over and took Benjy away. "We'll just have to go and talk to the Vicar. Your Mum'll do what's best, you can be sure of that. And she's got to give up her Sunday sit-down and walk all the way to Stradling because of it."

"Yes, you just think of that," said their

mother, "instead of flying at me like a wild cat. Now get your clothes on, do. You're going to be that late. And Benjy, you sit down and take up Baby; all this noise and commotion, no wonder she's woke."

6

"I'm not going to be shut up"

Sunday school was at Stradling, of course, in the
school by the church. Four times they walked
that way along the towpath on Sundays, and
there was always a hurry in the afternoon to get
back there after dinner. It was the worst of the
four journeys, when everybody felt full and
sleepy and in the mood to dawdle. But this
time Mouldy didn't notice the walk at all. She
had her mind full of that dreadful Brackley
workhouse.

They had to pass it on the way to market, a
gaunt grey building with hundreds of staring
little windows, inside a huge wall with ferocious
spikes on it. "The House", everybody called it,
a place for people with no one belonging to
them, too old or too poor or too ill to look after

44

themselves. It was used as a dreadful threat to children who didn't eat up their dinners or who wasted things or wore out their clothes too fast.

"If you carry on like this you'll have us all in The House," they said to them. The disgrace of going into The House would be terrible. But nobody from Canal Row ever had, and only once had Mouldy ever set eyes on anybody from there – a bunch of the children who had been allowed out for a treat, and poor hollow-eyed little things they had been, with clothes all exactly the same, and cropped hair.

In the catechism class that day, Mouldy sank right down to the very bottom, below even Sally Widcock and Clemmie Mason, the dunces who could never answer anything. But she didn't notice. If it had been Teacher who was taking the class there would have been trouble, but on Sundays it was Mrs Donaldson the Vicar's wife, and she was always kind.

"Is she feeling ill, do you know?" she asked the other girls, as Mouldy seemed unable to answer any question herself.

"She's bin reading too many books," said somebody.

45

"She's got an orphan at home," said some-body else, who knew a little more.

Mrs Donaldson shook her head. She didn't understand, but she didn't ask Mouldy any more.

When school was over, Mouldy was swept out in the jostle of children who were in a hurry to get home for tea. She stood in her outdoor clothes in the playground with May tugging at her.

"There's Mum over there, at the Vicarage."

Mouldy let May pull her over to the gravel sweep that went up to the Vicarage. It was Mum all right, on the Vicarage steps, she knew her hat and shawl. Standing by the open front door, talking to her, were the Vicar and Mr Gerald. Then behind them Mouldy saw some-thing that made her wrench her hand out of May's and run up the drive. She charged up the stone steps, dived behind Mr Gerald and seized Benjy.

"You're not going to take him to The House," she shouted, and started to drag him over the threshold.

It took her mother a moment or two to collect her wits. "Moll – ie Kippins!" She made an outraged grab at her. "You must be out of your mind. Leave hold of him at once."

Mr Gerald came down the steps and took Benjy's hand. "He's not going to the workhouse. We'll do our best for him, don't you worry. We're going to make some enquiries in Oxford. But until we've done that, he's going to stay here."

Mouldy clung on. "Billy and Georgie would make room for him in their big bed. And I don't mind having Flo in my lap when we're sitting at table. He hasn't got nobody to love him. We'd love him."

Mr Gerald looked back up the steps. The Vicar came forward. "We'll look after him till he goes. He can help in the stable and in the garden, and we'll see he gets plenty to eat."

"And I tell you what, young Mollie," said Mr Gerald, "when we take him back to Oxford, which is what we'll have to do in a few days, you can come with us and see him settled in. How about that?"

"Thank the Vicar and Mr Gerald, then," said Mrs Kippins reprovingly. "I'm sure it's very kind of you, Sir, when she's given so much trouble. It's those books that are to blame. She does nothing but read and she gets these odd fancies."

Through blinding tears, Mouldy looked up at the group standing by the front door. The Vicar and Mr Gerald didn't look stern, but kind. Benjy was drooping, dejected, bewildered.

"He loves our baby," said Mouldy.

"Well then, there's a baby here," said Mr Gerald. "I ought to know, I'm her uncle and her godfather."

There was no more to be said. Mouldy allowed herself to be led down the drive. She didn't even turn to wave goodbye to Benjy.

"She didn't ought to be taken to Oxford," said May self-righteously. "Not when she's bin so naughty. Did she, Mum?"

But Mrs Kippins said nothing, except to tell May sharply not to let Flo walk on the canal side of her when she was going down the tow-path.

"Where are they going to take Benjy then?"
persisted May.

"The Vicar and Mr Gerald know of a nice
home for poor boys in Oxford, where they'll be
kind to him and teach him a trade."

"What's a trade then?"

"Oh, carpentering or building or shoemaking.
Something where he can earn his own living,
instead of hanging round begging his bread.
He's a lucky boy to have that interest took in
him. They're going to write and say he's a
deserving case. So stop your crying, Mollie.
There's many who hasn't half so much as him."

"But in the home they sent Froggy to, he was
shut up," wept Mouldy. "Just once a year they
took them into the country for a treat. And
Benjy loves our baby."

"Well then, maybe he'll find a baby to love
there. Like your Froggy did. Remember what
you read to us?"

"But that's a book, Mum," objected May.
"That's not real."

"Oh, hold your hush, May Kippins, and stop
knowing everything. Just run off home, go on,

we've had enough of you. See the fire's good, and start making some toast. We'll have a treat today and open a pot of bramble jelly, and you, Mollie, you tuck your arm through mine and we'll keep each other warm."

7

Escape

That was Sunday. The days went past and nobody at home said anything about Benjy; nor did Mouldy ask, for fear of what she might hear. She spent playtime at school staring out towards the Vicarage, but there was not a glimpse of him. The other children sometimes called, "How's your orphan then?" but she didn't answer.

But on Friday she had the laugh on them. While the seniors were bent double over their slates trying to do their sums, and the babies were chanting their twice-times, and everybody was gloomy with the thought of there being at least two hours before playtime, Mr Gerald put his head round the school door and asked for Mollie Kippins.

"I told her she could come to Oxford when we took young Benjy there. Well, we've found him a nice place in the Philanthropic Boys' Home down in St Botolph's Road where he'll be as snug as a bug in a rug. So can I beg the day off for Mollie? I'll deliver her back before the end of school so that she can go home with the rest of the family. Off you skip, Mollie my girl; you'll find Benjy waiting outside in the dog-cart. We don't want to hang around in this frosty weather."

The Vicarage dog-cart stood in the road by the playground. Alf Hobbs, who was the odd-jobman, was holding the horse and he hoisted Mouldy into the back seat beside Benjy. Benjy was unnaturally neat and clean, quite different from the ragged, dirty, tousle-headed boy who had come home with her. She felt easy with him before; now she was shy. Was he minding what had happened? Was he blaming her?

"Did *they* give you them?" She touched his trousers.

"They got them from somebody who had a young gentleman same age as me. *And* boots too. *And* a jacket." He looked down at them with pride. Then his face got frightened. "What's this place they're going to now?"

Mouldy shook her head. "I didn't mean it like this," she said huskily. "Was they kind to you, back there?" She looked over her shoulder at the Vicarage.

"The lady, she was lovely. She let me look at the baby – they've got one too. The rest of them, they was kind enough. And you could eat till you didn't want no more – think of that, just."

Mr Gerald swung himself up into the front seat, Alf Hobbs climbing up beside him. "All right, you two? Then hold on tight, we don't want anybody spilling out before we get to the station."

After that Mouldy and Benjy said nothing. It would have been difficult to be heard, anyway, above the rattle of the cartwheels, and they had to hold tight to the little rail at the side of the cart to avoid being shaken out.

They clattered down the road that led from Stradling to the station, a road that Mouldy, who only walked the canal towpath, hardly knew. Facing backwards, they watched the tall church spire recede into the distance; they passed the last cottage that straggled on the outskirts, and were out in the open countryside, perched high above the hedges and looking down into the fields. There was the turning to Canal Row. Three more miles and they were at the station and were being lifted down, with legs so cold that Mouldy only knew she had reached the ground because she could go no further down.

"Looks as if it's blowing up for snow," said Mr Gerald. "Do you like snow, you two? Snowball fights and sliding and all that? All right, Alf, you take the dog-cart back home, but mind you're here to meet us at two o'clock. I want to get Mollie back to school. Now, Mr Jarvis, one return and two halves for Oxford, one of those halves to come back here, the other one a single."

It was a very different journey from the one a week before. The train sped on, taking them so far so fast. And only one of the two halves was going to come back. Mouldy stared out of the

55

window at the grim, slate-coloured sky. She could not bear to look at Benjy. At last he nudged her.

"See over there?" He pointed to a huge stretch of meadowland, dotted with the distant figures of cattle and horses. By the railway line there was first a canal, then willow trees, and then the flat land went on and on until it met the sky far away in the distance. "That's where I sleep sometimes."

"Down there?" said Mouldy, appalled. "But there's no houses."

"I found a shed. It's got hay in it. Mostly I can keep warm. And there's money to be got in Oxford if you knows the right places to stand and ask for it. Outside the colleges for one."

"Nearly at Oxford now," said Mr Gerald. "You both looking at the canal? That's your canal, Mollie. It follows the railway line and then goes off to the Canal Row and then Stradling. But I reckon you're glad you haven't got to walk all the way along it back home today."

But Mouldy's mind was on the shed. "Has it got windows?" she said to Benjy. "And a fireplace and that?"

"It's a shed, I'm telling you. Not a house."

"Back home there's a house," said Mouldy dreamily. "It's where a gamekeeper used to live, on the edge of a wood. But he died and there's no one in it now. And it's got a fireplace and an upstairs and a downstairs. Our Billy climbed in once and he told me." In her mind, she saw smoke coming out of the chimney, and a fire in the grate, and Benjy sitting in front of it . . .

The train was crawling now. "It's Oxford!" said Benjy, looking at the huddle of houses. He tugged at Mr Gerald's sleeve. "It's Oxford. Where are we going now?"

"Not far. Keep close to me, I don't want to lose you. Here, I'll carry your bundle."

He pushed the children through the jostle of the station. But Benjy was dragging, Mouldy could feel it. She knew he didn't want to get to wherever it was Mr Gerald was taking them, and Mr Gerald kept having to turn round and wait.

"You'll have to hurry, you two. I said we'd be there at twelve, and Mollie and I have a train to catch home."

They were in a street of dark high houses now, a street that went plunging downhill towards a big, grim building in the distance. Benjy stopped.

"I know that." He pointed. "That's the Orphan Boys."

"That's right," said Mr Gerald, cheerfully.

"That where I'm going?"

"That's it. Right in the middle of the town, so you won't feel cut off, will you?"

"Well I'm NOT, see!" shouted Benjy. In a flash he had turned and was running up the street again.

For a second Mouldy watched him, and then she ran too. "Benjy! Benjy!" she wailed, trying to see the fleeing figure dodging in and out of the people in the road. "Ben – jy," she panted as she turned the corner after him. There was no sign of him there. The street was empty of everyone, except a horse and cart plodding over the cobbles. "Benjy," she cried hopelessly, trotting down past more black houses with grubby doorsteps that came right down to the street.

"Stop your gab, can't you," said a fierce voice from inside a door.

"Benjy!" said Mouldy with a gasp.

"Stow it. Come on in then, quick."

She found herself in a dirty doorway. Inside a broken flight of stairs went up into darkness. An arm grabbed her and pulled her back against the wall, then the door was kicked shut. "Now keep quiet."

Nothing stirred in the house, nor was there any sound from the street outside. Mouldy pressed herself against the wall. Her heart was thumping so hard that she could feel her ribs shaking. "What are we waiting for?" she quavered at last.

"Till *he* goes away."

"Who goes?"

"That cove who wanted to put me *there*."

"It wasn't The House. He did promise."

"Nearest thing to it, then. I know those Orphan Boys. I seed them walking in the town, like prisoners in a line, all dressed the same. Sometimes me and my mates looks through the gates at 'em in their playground. Just like a prison it is, walls all round and not a tree, not a blade of grass, nothing. And bells to tell them when to stop and when to come in. And bars on the windows. Anything 'd be better than that."

"But Mr Gerald said they'd look after you. Teach you a trade," Mouldy said despairingly. She felt she had to show Benjy that she hadn't betrayed him, not completely.

"Daresay they would. But I'm not going to be shut up, see."

"Where are you going to go then?" said Mouldy at last.

"Back to Port Meadow."

"But it's *cold*." Mouldy remembered those bleak flat fields that stretched on forever, into the cold grey sky.

"Better'n the Orphan Boys. I'm off."

"I'm coming too, then."

Benjy didn't answer. He was pulling open the door and peering out. A second later he was gone. She followed. There he was, slithering like a shadow by the walls of the houses. It was hard to keep him in sight, he was forever darting down tiny lanes, twisting round corners. Mouldy panted after him. She lost count of the streets she crossed, she didn't notice where she was at all; her eyes were straining after that running, dodging figure. And then the houses stopped and they were in a lane like back home. There was nobody in sight and for the first time she dared to call.

"Benjy, wait for me."

He turned. "Dunno why you're coming."

"I'll help make you comfortable. Make a fire. I'm good at making fires, even Mum says that. I could cook too."

Benjy said nothing. He just walked on. Then he spoke. "I could go and get a few coppers in the town while you could be looking after the place a bit. Be nice to have someone out there to talk to, specially in the winter."

Mouldy nodded eagerly. "Oh yes, I'd do all that."

"Here we are then, we've got to go down here." He led the way over a bridge, climbed a fence and they were out on those huge fields.

"Out here?" Mouldy's courage failed for a moment. The wind was blowing at her and through her, making her clutch her arms round herself to try to keep the cold out.

"Over in those trees up here, that's where the hut is." Benjy led the way over the rough ground, the grass rimed with frost, the earth rutted and hard. "It's hid nicely. Nobody comes up here."

They followed the line of willows. On the other side, Mouldy could see the canal, the canal that went winding all the way back to Canal Row, Mr Gerald said. There was a black shape by the trees.

"There it is," said Benjy. "The door's got broke, but get into the hay inside and you can soon make yourself snug. It gets lonely though, so most nights I tries to find a mate with a bit of room to spare. (There's doorways in the town and railway trucks and boatyards, if you knows where to look.) Why then, some- body's come and mended the door. And they've put a lock on it!"

There was no doubt about that. The black shed with its corrugated iron roof now had its door firmly held by a huge padlock. Benjy gave it a kick; the door held. The children stared at it.

"We can't get in then," said Mouldy, aghast.

"Looks like it."

"What are we going to do then?"

"I dunno."

Shivering, Mouldy looked round her. She was frightened. She'd never been so far away from home, and she'd never stood in such a desolate empty space, a place where the sky seemed about to fall on her head, and where nobody seemed ever to have been – except that one enemy who had crept up secretly and shut Benjy's poor little house against him. More than anything, she wanted home and all of them around her. Suddenly she made up her mind.

"I'm going home, and you come too. That house I told you about, that one on the edge of the woods – well, you can go there. It's better than this by a long way, and I could make you comfortable, just see if I couldn't."

"How do we get there then?"

"Walk along the canal like Mr Gerald said."

"All that way!"

Mouldy quailed as she remembered all the frozen distance that the train had whirled them through, but she answered resolutely. "Doesn't matter. We'll get there sometime."

8

Lost in the snow

Hour after hour had gone by, and still they were plodding along the canal path, with never a sign of life in the fields that stretched around them. The light was fading, the wind was getting up, blowing freezing into their faces and making their eyes stream, and the sky was taking on a thick yellowish look. A flake, like a white feather, came twisting slowly down.

"Snow," said Benjy, stopping and peering up. "Looks like there's a lot up there."

"Come on then." Mouldy pulled at him.

At first they could almost count the flakes as they fell, but soon the air was thick with them; if they looked up at the sky it was speckled with dark shadows and their faces were covered with them. As it was, the wind drove snow into

Mouldy's eyes, and if she opened her mouth snow came in.

"There's something up there," said Benjy, pointing above the hedge. "Those your houses? Canal Row?"

Mouldy peered through the gloom and the swirling snow. "There's just railway up there. Our houses aren't by a railway."

"Then it's your station maybe."

"We could look."

On legs so stiff with cold that she could barely move them she followed Benjy up a steep bank, slithering on the snowy surface, grabbing at bushes to keep herself from falling back again. She landed on all fours in a lane above.

"It isn't our station. Not the junction."

It was just a corrugated iron shelter on a platform where somebody had lit a lamp and gone away again. Nobody was there and it didn't look as if anybody lived for miles around. But something about it was familiar; it was the place where the Other Lot had boarded the train on the pantomime day. She remembered the remarks the Canal Row children had made about cow sheds.

"It's miles and miles away," she said with horror. "We'd bin in that train for ages before we got here!"

Savagely, Benjy turned on her. "And you've brought me all this way for nothing! All this way from Oxford! That's twice you've done it, brought me out to nothing, worse than nothing. Back in the town there'd be somewhere to go out of the cold and I could have scrounged some vittles. I wish I'd never met up with you! And to think I nearly got away from you once and them as wanted to take me to the Orphan Boys, and then listened to you again and let you bring me here!" He made a gesture at the desolate little platform, now completely carpeted with snow, where nobody had trodden since the lamp had been lit.

Mouldy clutched frantically at his snow-encrusted arm. "It will be all right, honest it will. We've only got to go on walking, Mr Gerald said. I know the way, it's just that path down there; we keep going and we'll get there."

"Keep going and we'll fall into the water more like. How do we keep going in all this? Leave alone it's getting dark."

Desperate, Mouldy cast around for some way to coax him on. In her mind she could so plainly see that fire burning in the gamekeeper's grate and the two of them sitting beside it, snug and happy. It was just a matter of walking on, some time they'd get there; not tonight perhaps, but tomorrow. "Look, there's a seat inside that shelter, we could sit there a bit if you're tired, and then we could go on. If we pressed together we could get warmer; Mum and me do that sometimes."

Benjy allowed himself to be led up to the bench and huddled himself in the corner, against the iron wall. Mouldy pushed her hands up her coat sleeves and squeezed up against him. "I'll tell you a story. About the house we're going to live in."

Benjy said nothing. She peered at his face. He had his eyes shut and his shoulders hunched up round his ears. She went on; after all, he might be listening. "Well, this house is just outside a wood, there's a path up to it, but nobody goes. Billy took me there once. It's all shut up, but you can put a knife to open the catch of one of the windows, he showed me.

"Well, there's a downstairs room and a scullery off, and the downstairs room has a grate and an oven. Just think of that now, a proper oven! And there's wood, heaps of it, under the trees. You can pick up some of it and I'll lay the fire, and in a minute or two it'll go roaring away up the chimney, making all the room light so we won't need no candles.

"And I know where there's potatoes in clamps in one of the fields; Billy showed me. I'd fetch some of those and we'd put them in the ashes to roast. Think of that, a lovely, hot, roast potato – you can hold it in your hands to warm you, and stretch out your feet to the fire.

"It won't be all good and proper the first night, but next day it will. We can make some stools and a table – all the logs lying around, and there's plenty of straw in the stacks for mattresses. I daresay I could find a kettle and a saucepan maybe, and we could catch rabbits in the fields. And in the summer we could grow things in the garden, beans and things, because there's quite a bit of garden . . ." Her voice droned on and on. She forgot about the cold as she saw that house springing to life.

"What's that?" Benjy had sprung up from his corner and was leaning forward tensely. There was a rumble and a roar and lights shining through a dazzle of snow. "It's a train!" He looked wildly about him and made as if to bolt off. But it was too late; it was sweeping into the platform, slowing, stopping, with a hissing of steam. There was a clatter and somebody jumped down and stumped up the platform, footsteps muffled by snow.

"You two getting on this train?"

Dumbly, Mouldy stared at the uniformed man confronting them.

"Where are you going then? It's no night for youngsters like you to be out – back of beyond place like this too. Where do you come from?"

"Canal Row," quavered Mouldy.

"Where's that then?"

She searched her numbed brain. "Stradling, it's near."

"Stradling? You want King's Norton for that, and it's a good march from there, isn't it? Look sharp, train's late already." He pulled open a door. Mouldy hesitated for a second, and then, pulling at Benjy, she clambered in. And then the train started again.

Outside were white sheets of snow; inside, the snow fell off their clothes and lay on the wooden slats of the seats, dripping on to the floor. Mouldy could feel the wheels gathering speed, the train was flying over the miles; it thought nothing of the wind, the cold, the distance. Why, at this rate they'd be home within minutes! Her spirits soared.

"It won't take long now. Then there's a bit of a walk to Canal Row, then over the fields and we're there and I can start getting you warm."

Benjy, who was clutching the strap of the window and pulling as if he was trying to stop a runaway horse, turned and shouted at her. "You and your bit of a walk and over the fields! How're we going to get there with everything covered with snow! Look at it all outside!"

He pointed to the white wastes that shone through the dark. "Nothing there, but snow. Not a house, not a shed, nothing. Back in the town there's always somewhere out of the weather. Start getting me warm! How do you set about finding sticks when you can't even see them?"

Mouldy looked at him with trembling lips. The bright vision of the home and the comfort she was going to bring Benjy was melting away like the snow under their feet. Despairingly she tried to cling to it. " I *promise*. We'll be so snug, you and me. Just a little while," she pleaded.

"Promise!" he said contemptuously.

The train stopped. Somebody padded over the platform outside, tugged open the door. "King's Norton. Here you are. Mr Jarvis, you take over these young 'uns and sort them out. I dunno whether they got tickets or not, but one thing I do know, they oughtn't to be out and about on a night like this." A whistle blew, a uniformed figure jumped back into the moving train, and they were left, staring at the lighted windows that were sliding past them.

A voice by them made them jump. "Well, who are you anyway and where did you come from?" A hand fell on Mouldy's shoulder. Behind them was a shadowy figure in a peaked cap. Benjy wrenched himself away. Floundering over the snow, he had disappeared into the darkness before Mouldy had realized what was happening. Then she too tried to struggle free.

"Benjy – you don't know the way! Wait, Benjy, I'm coming!"

But the hand held her there. "You're the lot they're looking for. The telegrams that've bin coming through on my machine! And every time the porter having to walk with 'em in this weather all the way up to Stradling Vicarage. He's gone now with the latest. But I've cotched you, and you're staying."

Mouldy wasn't listening. "Benjy, come back, you don't know where it is, you'll get lost." She turned and tried to pull the stationmaster's hand away.

"Steady now, it's no good you carrying on like that. You stay with me until they can send for someone to collect you. The Vicarage cart is coming over from Stradling to meet the next down train and pick up the gentleman who's bin doing all the telegraphing from Oxford. They can take you home. It's no night for you to be traipsing over the roads."

"But there's Benjy," sobbed Mouldy. "He's out there in all the snow, he doesn't know where to go, and I *promised*."

"You can sit by my fire then and I'll have a bit of a look around."

She had no more strength in her. She dragged numb feet over the snow, and found herself pushed into a small room, with a smoky oil lamp and a sulky fire and a litter of packages tossed everywhere. Her knees gave way under her, and she crouched on the gritty floor. A few minutes later, the stationmaster tramped in and banged the door behind him.

"Not a sign, leastways, not as far as I'm prepared to go through in all this."

Tears poured down Mouldy's face. "I said this time it would be all right." She was sitting on the dirty floor now, her back propped up against a wooden crate.

"You'll have to tell the Vicarage people that then, when they come. Nobody's going out from here to look. I can't leave the station, the porter's still out, and I'm not letting you go. Still, I'd better telegraph through to Oxford; at least they needn't go on looking for you there."

He sat down at a table littered with bits of paper. Through her sobs, Mouldy could hear the clicking of his machine. She fell into a stupor; sometimes there were voices; sometimes the door slammed; feet came and went; but she never lifted her head. Then somebody pulled her to her feet.

"Mollie Kippins!" She stood there, swaying, hardly able to open her eyes. "Thank heavens I've got one of you, at any rate. Thank you very much, Mr Jarvis, for taking charge. Yes, you did quite right to keep her. We'll take her back to Canal Row."

It seemed to be Mr Gerald who was there, and who lifted her up into the dog-cart and pulled a rug round her. She came to life as the wheels moved. "Benjy! He's out there somewhere!" She pointed wildly over the fields. "I was going to take him where it was all warm and comfortable, and now I've lost him. He won't never be able to believe me now."

"Let's get you home first, and then Alf Hobbs and I can start looking. One thing, we'll be able to see tracks in this snow, and we'll keep a look-out as we go."

Wedged in between Mr Gerald and Alf Hobbs, Mouldy at first tried to strain her eyes along the road, but soon fell back into her doze, swaying from side to side, her head slumping first on one shoulder, then on the other.

The wheels had stopped, there were voices, but she didn't want to listen. Mr Gerald was talking, explaining, but there seemed to be her father there too. She was lifted down and she struggled to unstick her eyelids. There she was, in the doorway at home and everybody was crowding round.

"It's all right, Mum," May was calling. "She's safe. Mr Gerald's brought her home."

Flo was tugging at her, butting her head against her, wailing. "We thought you was lost, forever and ever – like one of those norphans."

Mouldy's senses came back. "Benjy – I've got to look for him!"

"He's here!" said May. "Didn't you hear nothing of what Daddy and Mr Gerald was saying?"

"Leave the poor child be." Her mother came forward. "Can't you see she's all of a daze? Come along, my Moll, and you, May, fetch the

tin bath. Daddy'll lift the kettle down and we'll get the shoes and stockings off her and her feet into some warm water before anything else."

She was pushed forward. There was Benjy, wrapped in Mum's old shawl, sitting in front of the fire, bare feet stretched out to the comforting blaze. He looked up at her, shame-faced.

"I would've come back to look for you, like your Dad was going to, but they took away my boots."

"The railway porter found him," announced May. "He'd been to the Vicarage with a telegram and he was going back to the station and he found Benjy."

Appalled, Mouldy hung her head. She couldn't look him in the face. For a third time she had let him down, let him be caught. And hadn't she promised? "Need he be going back to the Orphan Boys' this time? He thinks it's a prison. There's a little house. Billy knows of it too, don't you, Billy? I'm sure there's nobody as wants it. We could ask, anyway. Nobody need see him, and sometimes maybe I could take our baby there for him."

Her father tumbled her hair. "He's staying,

Mollie, my lass. I reckon Providence means us to have him, the way he's come back like this. None of us would like being shut up. Happen we shouldn't have sent him off in the first place. The Vicarage can find work for him, I daresay, and he can sleep and feed with us."

"Here's going to be his *home*? His real home?" said Mouldy, marvelling.

"Tell you what – I'll make him a stool. Come Sunday, I'll make him his own stool."

Billy pressed on to more important matters. "Now Mum, can we have them potato cakes? You said when they was all safe and warm and dry, we could have potato cakes."